MAMA LOU'S BELLY

MARIE-FRANCINE HÉBERT

illustrated by
GUILLAUME PERREAULT

ORCA BOOK PUBLISHERS

Who is that hiding
in Mama Lou's belly?

Everyone is wondering.

Hello, it's me!

says the little voice
inside Mama Lou's belly.
But no one hears it.

One of the neighborhood birds watches Mama Lou and chirps.
He's very afraid a cat might be hiding in there.

"Why do I think that?
They spend so much time petting her belly."

"They already have one house cat
who tries to eat me!
Soon there will be two of them.
Poor me!"

That's nonsense!
You're being a birdbrain.

says the small voice
inside Mama Lou's belly.
But no one hears it.

Snuggled up against Mama Lou's belly, the cat purrs.
She's convinced she knows what's going on in there,
because Mama Lou has been craving cheese.

"It's a big juicy mouse!
And it won't fly away like that bird
when I try to catch it. Mmm!
What a feast that will be."

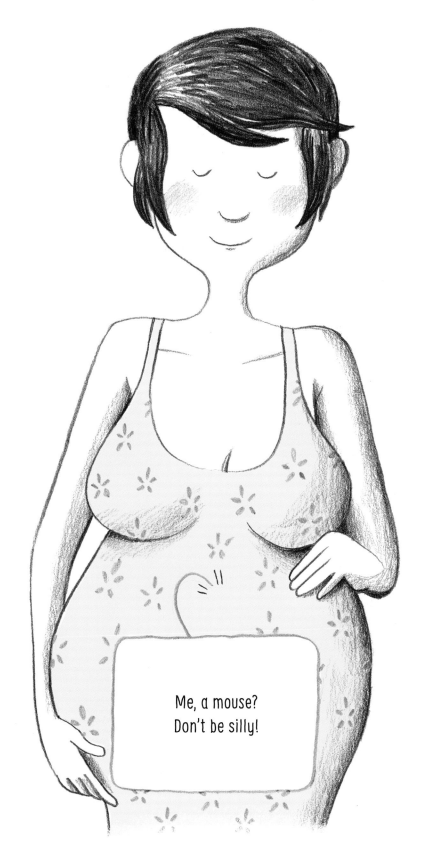

says the small voice
inside Mama Lou's belly.
But no one hears it.

The ball, which spends a lot of time alone in the corner,
gets really excited when it sees Mama Lou's belly.

"It's easy to guess what's growing inside.
Another ball, of course!"

"Finally I'll have a friend to play with!
I can already imagine how it'll look.
Pink, blue, green or orange...
with stripes, lines, squares or polka dots..."

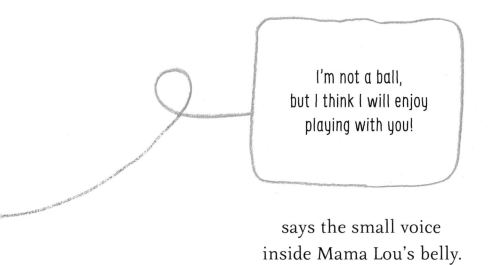

I'm not a ball,
but I think I will enjoy
playing with you!

says the small voice
inside Mama Lou's belly.
But no one hears it.

Mama and Daddy are sure
it's a baby hiding in her belly.
They can even feel it move.
The whole family is thrilled.

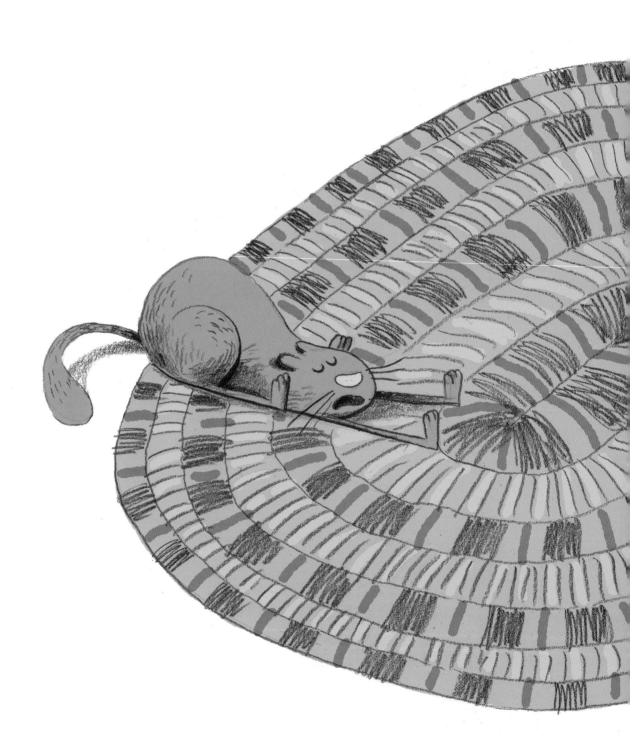

"A boy, obviously," says the older brother.
"And judging by his kicks,
he already knows how to play soccer.
He'll be great on my team!"

"We'll know who it is when it's born,"
say Mama and Daddy.

"I want you to be a boy! Please!"
begs the older brother, and he covers
his mother's belly with kisses.

It's too dark in
here—I can't see
if I'm a boy.

says the small voice
inside Mama Lou's belly.
But no one hears it.

"Well, *I* want you to be a girl! Please!" begs the older sister.
"You'll be my doll. I'll dress you up and do your hair.
And I'll have to teach you everything,
because a baby like you doesn't know anything.
But don't worry—I'll tell you what to do."

I know at least one thing.
I'm not a doll!

says the small voice
inside Mama Lou's belly.
But no one hears it.

"I hope the baby has its mom's rosy cheeks
and its dad's twinkly eyes," says Grandma.

"I hope it's not as bald as me," adds Grandpa.

The family laughs.

"Expecting a baby is like being given a gift," says Daddy.

"You can't wait to see what it is!" finishes Mama.

Everyone agrees.
Except for the baby.

A cat,
a mouse,
a ball,
a soccer player,
a doll,
a gift and what else?!
That's enough!
I'm *me*!
Don't you understand?

says the small voice
inside Mama Lou's belly.
But no one hears it.

Tired of being ignored,
the baby decides it's time to be heard.
When they are born, they let out a loud cry.

"WAAAAAA!"

Mama and Daddy gaze in awe.
Grandma and Grandpa too.
And the baby *does* have rosy cheeks
and twinkly eyes and is as bald as Grandpa.

"What a sweetheart," they say, over and over.

"It will be a while before
we can start playing with the baby,"
says the older brother.

"The only thing they know
how to do is ask for milk."

"Or for hugs," adds the older sister.

"Just like you two when you were born,"
Mama and Daddy remind them.

"See you later, baby!"
shout the brother and the sister.

Text copyright © Marie-Francine Hébert 2023
Illustrations copyright © Guillaume Perreault 2015
Translation copyright © Charles Simard 2023

Published in Canada and the United States in 2023 by Orca Book Publishers.
Le bedon de madame Loubidou © 2015 Marie-Francine Hébert, Guillaume
Perreault and les Éditions Les 400 coups Montreal (Quebec) Canada
orcabook.com

Library and Archives Canada Cataloguing in Publication
Title: Mama Lou's belly / Marie-Francine Hébert ;
illustrations by Guillaume Perreault.
Other titles: Bedon de madame Loubidou. English
Names: Hébert, Marie-Francine, author. | Perreault, Guillaume, 1985- illustrator.
Description: Translation of: Le bedon de madame Loubidou.
Identifiers: Canadiana (print) 20220436444 |
Canadiana (ebook) 20220436452 | ISBN 9781459833883 (hardcover) |
ISBN 9781459833890 (PDF) | ISBN 9781459833906 (EPUB)
Classification: LCC PS8565.E2 B4213 2023 | DDC jC843/.54—dc23

Library of Congress Control Number: 2022947181

Summary: In this illustrated picture book, everybody is guessing
what's in Mama Lou's belly. The bird thinks it could be a cat, the
cat thinks it might be a mouse and the sister thinks it could
be a doll. But only the baby knows who they truly are!

Orca Book Publishers is committed to reducing the consumption of
nonrenewable resources in the production of our books. We make
every effort to use materials that support a sustainable future.

Orca Book Publishers gratefully acknowledges the support for its publishing
programs provided by the following agencies: the Government of Canada,
the Canada Council for the Arts and the Province of British Columbia
through the BC Arts Council and the Book Publishing Tax Credit.

We acknowledge the financial support of the Government of Canada
through the National Translation Program for Book Publishing, an
initiative of the *Roadmap for Canada's Official Languages 2013-2018:
Education, Immigration, Communities*, for our translation activities.

Cover and interior artwork by Guillaume Perreault
Translated by Charles Simard

Printed and bound in South Korea.

26 25 24 23 • 1 2 3 4

To my daughter, Lou,
and my granddaughter,
Billie, who inspired this story.
M.-F.H.

For Arthur, Roxanne and Julien.
G.P.